First published in 2008 by Simply Read Books
www.simplyreadbooks.com

Cataloging in Publication Data
Porter, Matthew, 1974-
        Monkey world / Matthew Porter.
ISBN 978-1-894965-95-8
        1. Monkeys–Juvenile poetry. 2. Alphabet rhymes.
I. Title.
PS3616.O7825M6 2008   j811'.6   C2008-900659-3

Book design by Robin Mitchell-Cranfield for hundreds & thousands

Printed in Singapore

10 9 8 7 6 5 4 3 2 1

Monkey World

Dedicated to my brother

Matthew Porter

Monkey World

An A–Z of Occupations

Simply Read Books

When flying to a distant moon,
You don't eat breakfast with a spoon.

In rockets high in outer space,
Things can float from place to place.

Scrambled eggs and crumbs from cakes
Hang in the air like soft snowflakes.

When astronauts fancy a bite,
They always chew with mouths shut tight.

If they were to munch and shout,
Bits of food might float out.

Aa

Astronaut

He tried to learn the bongos,
The piano and the spoons;
But not once did he manage
To play a single tune.

He tried to play the banjo,
Ukulele and guitar;
But he was never able
To strum a single bar.

Then he tried a double bass,
And it went very well;
He did a little plucking,
And it sounded really swell.

Bb

Bass

Home is the saddle,
To the heart that loves travel,
To the cowboy who rides the dirt trail.

Each day is a battle,
To round up the cattle,
And keep them from losing their way.

No shade for shelter,
In the terrible swelter,
No escaping the heat of the day.

Still on he must ride,
Through scorched countryside,
On the horse that is pebble-dash grey.

The stars and the moon
Will be shining bright soon,
As the night draws the sunlight away.

Then coyotes will prowl,
And wild wolves will howl,
At the cowboy who rides the dirt trail.

Cc

Cowboy

I solve the riddles and the muddles;
Follow footprints into puddles;
Hunt for clues among the grass;
With my magnifying glass.

There is no thief I cannot catch;
I have yet to meet my match;
My methods are most effective;
I'm a truly great detective!

Dd

Detective

He drives the engine with great pride
Across the country far and wide;
He shovels coal to build up steam
Then lets the engine's whistle scream.

The train moves slowly from the station
To much excited conversation;
Through the tunnel and over the bridge,
Along the winding mountain ridge.

The passengers all start swaying,
To rhythms the tracks are playing;
Through the hills into the valley,
There's no time to dilly-dally.

The train is heading for the coast,
As the proud driver begins to boast
And says, exactly on the chime,
He always gets them there on time!

Ee

Engine Driver

A firefighter's job might be
To rescue a cat perched up a tree;
Or to set those people free
Who fall down wells they do not see.

A firefighter's job might be
To climb a ladder carefully
And, at the top, proclaim with glee,
"False alarm! Just burnt pastry!"

A firefighter's job might be
To douse a burning factory;
Or, one day, alternatively,
To save the likes of you or me.

Ff

Firefighter

A robber who was not so bright,
Talked a bit too much one night;
And told a gangster pal his plan
To break into an armored van.

In jail the gangster struck a deal:
For time off, he agreed to squeal.
To the police this old friend told
How the robbery would unfold.

Inside the van some police hid,
And waited for the hijack bid.
They all looked rather funny,
Dressed as piles of paper money.

And as the robber grabbed the loot,
A cop yelled, "Stop, or I'll shoot!"
And then he knew to his disgust
A gangster's one you cannot trust.

Gg

Gangster

Lula is a hula hooper;
Her red hoop she thinks is super.
Lula loves her poodle, too.
They stick together just like glue.

When Lula goes to town for soup,
She always brings her hula hoop.
It often spins around her neck,
When dancing at the discotheque.

And as she strolls the avenue,
It's like a musical revue,
With the poodle and hula hoop,
Still spinning as she scoops up poop!

Hh

Hula Hooper

He invented a robot
To help do the mopping;
To wash dirty dishes;
And carry the shopping.

It cooked all his meals
And ironed his shirts,
And often surprised him
With tasty desserts.

Then one day the robot
Feeling slightly bored
Pulled out a wire
From its circuit board.

It stopped doing chores
And turned rather arty;
It repainted the house
And then threw a party!

Ii

Inventor

He mops the floor in the canteen
Where secret agents have just been;
And finds the journal of a queen;
And blueprints for a submarine.

It's not all finding diamond rings
Or messages from long lost kings.
Some day there's only sprinklings
Of soggy fries and onion rings.

The janitor extraordinaire
Will tidy any mess with flare.
He sees the ketchup on the chair
Before you even know it's there!

Jj

Janitor

There once was a king
Who dearly loved pies.
He gobbled portions
Of enormous size.

He'd wolf down the lot
Then belch in delight
At the wonderful pies
He'd tasted that night.

He'd undo his belt
Then politely implore
One of his servants
To fetch him some more.

Kk

King

I was boating in the park,
When suddenly it got dark.
Freezing rain began to pour,
And I drifted far from shore.

Strong waves rocked the boat about,
Swooped me up and flung me out.
Franticly, I'm heard to shout
For the lifeguard to get me out!

LI

Lifeguard

The world's best magician,
Named Oscar Smidge-Widgeon,
Can pluck a pigeon from thin air.

A rabbit from a hat,
Or a fat ginger cat,
He can conjure while combing his hair.

With a sleight of the hands,
He can turn marching bands
Into lines of dancing iguanas.

And it's really no sweat,
To escape from a net,
Hung over a pool of piranhas.

With a flash of bright light,
He can vanish from sight,
And the crowd is left none the wiser.

(But don't ask him for change,
Or he might turn strange.
I've heard he's a bit of a miser!)

Mm

Magician

Writing an ode to a marmoset;
Or catching butterflies in a net;
Timing a spider climbing a wall;
Or recording a rare bird call;

Assessing an ant's lifting power;
Or counting petals on a flower;
Watching a beetle wrestle a leaf;
Or schools of fish circling a reef;

Finding a tiny, croaking frog;
Or intriguing fungi on a log;
Getting stuck in mud and mist:
Is jolly fun for a naturalist!

Nn

Naturalist

Officer Shirley walks her beat
In warm sunshine and freezing sleet.
She never has time to grab a seat
And take the weight off her poor feet.

When Shirley needs a special treat,
She books a pedicure replete;
With fancy oils that smell so sweet
And tingle lightly on her feet!

Oo

Officer

Pirate Captain Black Jack Morgan
Found inside a barrel organ
A map on which X marked the spot
Where buried treasure might be got.

And so he told his cut-throat crew
About the gold they'd now pursue;
And each and every man in turn
Thought of the riches he would earn.

Not long had they sailed from shore
When heavy rain began to pour,
And giant waves with pounding force
Pushed their battered boat off course.

They drifted through uncharted seas
Where monsters lurk and wait to seize;
To drag lost boats down to the deep,
Where sailors find eternal sleep.

An octopus with arms extending,
Wrapped itself around the rigging
And pulled the boat down to its doom
In the dark, foreboding gloom.

So now they lay with all the riches,
Of the coral and the fishes,
Far beneath the wicked waves
That beckon sailors to their graves.

Pp

Pirate

One day a queen squashed a pea,
While making sure no one could see;
And grinning with mischievous glee,
From the crime scene she did flee.

For the pea crushed on the floor,
She blamed a tired troubadour
Who swore he'd never seen before
The pea that lay upon the floor.

"You will have to lose you head,
Before this day is through," she said,
"For disregarding where you tread,
Like an utter dunder-head!"

When time came for the blade to fall,
Her majesty let out a call,
Then, giggling, she began to squall
About the best joke of them all.

The troubadour was unimpressed,
But knew better than to protest;
For he was just a lowly guest,
So faked amusement at the jest!

Qq

Queen

My sister loves to roller skate;
About it she is potty.
She thinks she is a roller girl
And acts all tough and snotty!

My sister says a roller girl,
When skating in a match,
Does whatever it takes to win;
She's quite prepared to scratch!

I tend to stay away from her,
When she puts on her skates.
I really much prefer to watch
Safely behind the gates!

Rr

Roller Girl

He knows what lullabies to play
To make the deadly snakes obey.
He plays soothing melodies
Meant to hypnotize and tease.

With every enchanting note
He wraps a finger round the throat
Of the venomous cobra snake
That rises up and starts to shake.

From side to side the cobra sways,
Like in a trance or foggy haze.
The snake charmer is not afraid;
He knows his flute must be obeyed.

Ss

Snake Charmer

I used to live next door
To a famous trumpet player.
In those days he was poor,
And worked as a bricklayer.

He practiced every night;
He certainly wasn't lazy.
But I couldn't fall asleep.
The music drove me crazy!

Fingers, pillows, earplugs –
I tried these and other things.
I phoned him over ninety times,
But he never heard the rings.

The trumpeteer from next door
Moved out of his apartment.
He got a record deal and tour,
And I got blissful silence.

Tt

Trumpet Player

The boys and girls are swaying,
To the ukulele playing,
On the breezes gently blowing
Across the bay.

In the trees, the birds are squawking,
But soon they all stop talking
As they hear the ukulele start to play.

The fishermen mend netting,
As the sun is slowly setting,
On the waves gently lapping
Across the bay.

In the grass, the geckos are napping,
But soon their feet are tapping,
As they love to hear the ukulele play.

Uu

Ukelele Player

He once drove a big, red tractor
But soon left to be an actor.
Sadly, he was not much good;
He acted like a piece of wood.

But entertainment was his dream,
So he thought up a clever scheme.
He bought a small wooden dummy
And learned about ventriloquy.

He practiced long into the night
To say such words as dynamite
Until, without moving his lips
He could say, "Nice sailing ships!"

Though he was only made of wood,
The new dummy was rather good.
And now the crowds don't ever bore
When those two planks go out on tour!

Vv

Ventriloquist

Grandpa used to be a wrestler,
At least, that's what he said.
"I threw people around a ring,
And broke chairs on my head!"

Grandma says he was a waiter,
And we've all been misled.
"He worked in a restaurant!"
Is what my grandma said.

Grandpa was a wrestling waiter,
I think that's what they said?
He wrestled all the diners
While they waited to be fed!

Ww

Wrestler

If you play the saxophone,
You can say you play the sax.
If you play the xylophone,
Then that won't cut the wax.

If you play the piano,
You are tinkling the keys.
And if you have to spell it,
It's really quite a breeze.

But if you play the xylophone,
No one will understand
When you say "I play the xylo,
In my school's marching band!"

Xx

Xylophonist

My mom is always super-stressed,
Even when it's sunny.
If you ask, "How was your day?"
She'll always answer, "Crummy."

She often moans about the bills
That pile up on the mat.
When we go on holiday,
She worries about our cat.

She says her job is worse than dull;
She wishes she was fired.
She says she hates all of her clothes
And whines when she is tired.

Today, my mom is acting strange;
She's dressed up in a toga.
She's behaving calm and sweet;
She must have started yoga.

Yy

Yoga Instructor

On a piece of paper, I began to draw a zoo.
I started with a panda, and a stick of bamboo.
Then I drew an alligator, dancing a tango;
Followed by a caterpillar, munching on a mango.

Next I drew a sea lion, clapping its flippers,
And a toucan, on a chair, sliding into slippers.
Then I drew a stick insect, under an umbrella;
And a sad, lonesome frog, singing a cappella.

Then I drew a tiger, sleeping quietly in bed,
And a beaver with a fever, baking loaves of bread.
Then I drew a penguin, with a slick hairdo;
And, of course, I had to draw a boxing kangaroo.

Next I drew a rabbit, riding on a scooter,
And a pelican, typing on a laptop computer.
Last, I drew a turtle, tucked up in its shell;
And a zookeeper, to make sure all is well.

Zz

Zoo Keeper